GEORGE BARNWELL.

A TRAGEDY, IN FIVE ACTS.

BY GEORGE LILLO.

Characters represented:

Covent Garden, 1825.

THOROWGOOD	-	-	-	Mr. Egerton.
UNCLE	-	-	-	-	Mr. Chapman
GEORGE BARNWELL	-	-	-	Mr. Cooper.
TRUEMAN	-	-	-	Mr. Baker.
BLUNT	-	-	-	-	Mr. Atkins.
JAILOR	-	-	-	-	Mr. Louis.
MILLWOOD	-	-	-	-	Mrs. Faucit.
LUCY	-	-	-	-	Mrs. Gibbs.
MARIA	-	-	-	-	Miss Jones.

ACT I.

SCENE I.—*A Room in Thorowgood's House.*

Enter THOROWGOOD *and* TRUEMAN.

True. Sir, the packet from Genoa is arrived,

(*Gives letters.*)

Thor. Heaven be praised, the storm that threatened our royal mistress, pure religion, liberty, and laws, is for a time diverted; by which means time is gained to make such preparations on our part as may, heaven concurring, prevent his malice, or turn the meditated mischief on himself.

True. He must be insensible indeed who is not affected when the safety of his country is concerned. Sir, may I know by what means—if I am too bold—

Thor. Your curiosity is laudable; and at some future period I shall gratify it with the greater pleasure, because from thence you may learn how honest merchants, as such, may sometimes contribute to the safety of their country, as they do at all times to its happiness; that if hereafter you should be tempted to any action that has the appearance of vice or meanness in it, upon reflecting on the dignity of our profession, you may with honest scorn reject whatever is unworthy of it.

True. Should Barnwell or I, who have the benefit of your example, by our ill conduct bring any imputation on that honourable name, we must be left without excuse.

Thor. You compliment, young man.— (TRUEMAN *bows respectfully*)—Nay, I am not offended. As the name of merchant never degrades the gentleman, so by no means does it exclude him; only take heed not to purchase the character of complaisance at the expense of your sincerity.

True. Well, sir, have you any commands for me at this time?

Thor. Only to look carefully over the files, to see if there are any tradesman's bills unpaid; and if there are to send and discharge them. We must not let artificers lose their time, so useful to the public and their families, in unnecessary attendance. [*Exit* TRUEMAN.

Enter MARIA.

Thor. Well, Maria, have you given orders for the entertainment? I would have it in some measure worthy the guests. Let there be plenty, and of the best; that the courtiers, though they should deny us citizens politeness, may at least commend our hospitality.

Maria. Sir, I have endeavoured not to wrong your well-known generosity by an ill-timed parsimony.

Thor. Nay, 'twas a needless caution; I have no cause to doubt your prudence.

Maria. Sir, I find myself unfit for conversation at present: I should but increase the

1

number of the company, without adding to their satisfaction.

Thor. Nay, my child, this melancholy must not be indulged.

Maria. Company will but increase it. I wish you would dispense with my absence; solitude best suits my present temper.

Thor. You are not insensible that it is chiefly on your account these noble lords do me the honour so frequently to grace my board; should you be absent, the disappointment may make them repent their condescension, and think their labour lost.

Maria. He that shall think his time or honour lost in visiting you, can set no real value on your daughter's company, whose only merit is that she is yours. The man of quality, who chooses to converse with a gentleman and merchant of your worth and character, may confer honour by so doing, but he loses none.

Thor. Come, come, Maria, I need not tell you that a young gentleman may prefer your conversation to mine, yet intend me no disrespect at all; for though he may lose no honour in my company, 'tis very natural for him to expect more pleasure in yours. I remember the time when the company of the greatest and wisest man in the kingdom would have been insipid and tiresome to me, if it had deprived me of an opportunity of enjoying your mother's.

Maria. Yours, no doubt, was as agreeable to her: for generous minds know no pleasure in society but where 'tis mutual.

Thor. Thou know'st I have no heir, no child but thee; the fruits of many years successful industry must all be thine; now it would give me pleasure great as my love, to see on whom you would bestow it. I am daily solicited by men of the greatest rank and merit for leave to address you; but I have hitherto declined it, in hopes that by observation I should learn which way your inclination tends; for as I know love to be essential to happiness in the married state, I had rather my approbation should confirm your choice than direct it.

Maria. What can I say?—how shall I answer as I ought this tenderness, so uncommon, in the best of parents? But you are without example; yet, had you been less indulgent, I had been most wretched. That I look on the crowd of courtiers that visit here with equal esteem, but equal indifference, you have observed, and I must needs confess; yet, had you asserted your authority, and insisted on a parent's right to be obeyed, I had submitted, and to my duty sacrificed my peace.

Thor. From your perfect obedience in every other instance, I feared as much, and therefore would leave you without a bias in an affair wherein your happiness is so immediately concerned.

Maria. Whether from a want of that just

ambition that would become your daughter, or from some other cause, I know not; but I find high birth and titles do not recommend the man who owns them to my affections.

Thor. I would not that he should, unless his merit recommends him more. A noble birth and fortune, though they make not a bad man good, yet they are a real advantage to a worthy one, and place his virtues in the fairest light.

Maria. I cannot answer for my inclinations, but they shall ever be submitted to your wisdom and authority; and as you will not compel me to marry where I cannot love, so love shall never make me act contrary to my duty. Sir, have I your permission to retire?

Thor. I'll see you to your chamber.

[*Exeunt.*

SCENE II.—*A Room in Millwood's House.*

MILLWOOD *discovered;* LUCY *waiting.*

Mil. How do I look to-day, Lucy?

Lucy. O, killingly, madam! a little more red, and you'll be irresistible! But why this more than ordinary care of your dress and complexion? What new conquest are you aiming at?

Mill. A conquest would be new indeed!

Lucy. Not to you, who make 'em every day,—but to me. Well, 'tis what I'm never to expect,—unfortunate as I am: but your wit and beauty—

Mill. First made me a wretch, and still continue me so. Men, however generous or sincere to one another, are all selfish hypocrites in their affairs with us. We are no otherwise esteemed or regarded by them, but as we contribute to their satisfaction. It is a general maxim among the knowing part of mankind, that a woman without virtue, like a man without honour, or honesty, is capable of any action, though never so vile: and yet what pains will they not take, what arts not use, to seduce us from our innocence, and make us contemptible and wicked, even in their own opinions? Then is it not just the villains, to their cost, should find us so? But guilt makes them suspicious, and keeps them on their guard; therefore we can take advantage only of the young and innocent part of the sex, who, having never injured women, apprehend no injury from them.

Lucy. Ay, they must be young indeed.

Mill. Such a one, I think, I have found. As I've passed through the city, I have often observed him receiving and paying considerable sums of money: from thence I conclude he is employed in affairs of consequence.

Lucy. Is he handsome?

Mill. Ay, ay, the stripling is well made.

Lucy. About—

Mill. Eighteen.

Lucy. Innocent, handsome, and about eighteen!—you'll be vastly happy. Why, if you manage well, you may keep him to yourself these two or three years.

Mill. If I manage well, I shall have done with him much sooner. Having long had a design on him, and meeting him yesterday, I made a full stop, and gazing wishfully on his face, asked him his name: he blushed, and bowing very low, answered—George Barnwell. I begged his pardon for the freedom I had taken, and told him that he was the person I had long wished to see, and to whom I had an affair of importance to communicate, at a proper time and place. He named a tavern; I talked of honour and reputation, and invited him to my house: he swallowed the bait, promised to come, and this is the time I expect him. (*knocking at the door*) Somebody knocks:—d'ye hear, I am at home to nobody to-day but him.—(*exit* LUCY)—Less affairs must give way to those of more consequence; and I am strangely mistaken if this does not prove of great importance to me and him too before I have done with him. Now, after what manner shall I receive him?—Let me consider—what manner of person am I to receive? He is young, innocent, and bashful; therefore I must take care not to put him out of countenance at first. But then, if I have any skill in physiognomy, he is amorous, and, with a little assistance will soon get the better of his modesty. I'll trust to nature, who does wonders in these matters. If to seem what one is not, in order to be the better liked for what one really is; if to speak one thing and mean the direct contrary, be art in a woman, then I know nothing of nature.

Enter BARNWELL, *bowing low;* LUCY *at a distance.*

Mill. Sir!—the surprise and joy!—
Barn. Madam!
Mill. This is such a favour.—(*advancing.*)
Barn. Pardon me, madam,—
Mill. So unhoped for, (*still advances:* BARNWELL *salutes her, and retires in confusion.*)—To see you here—excuse the confusion—
Barn. I fear I am too bold.
Mill. Alas, sir, all my apprehensions proceed from the fear of your thinking me so. Please, sir, to sit.—I am as much at a loss how to receive this honour as I ought, as I am surprised at your goodness in confering it.
Barn. I thought you had expected me—I promised to come.
Mill. This is the more surprising; few men are such religious observers of their word.
Barn. All who are honest are.
Mill. To one another; but we silly women are seldom thought of consequence enough to gain a place in your remembrance. (*laying her hand on his, as by accident.*)
Barn. Her disorder is so great, she don't perceive she has laid her hand on mine.—

Heaven, how she trembles! What can this mean? (*aside.*)

Mill. The interest I have in all that relates to you, (the reason of which you shall know hereafter) excites my curiosity; and, were I sure you would pardon my presumption, I should desire to know your real sentiments on a very particular affair.

Barn. Madam, you may command my poor thoughts on any subject: I have none that I would conceal.

Mill. You'll think me bold?
Barn. No, indeed.
Mill. What then are your thoughts of love?
Barn. If you mean the love of women, I have not thought of it at all. My youth and circumstances make such thoughts improper in me yet. But, if you mean the general love we owe mankind, I think no one has more of it in his temper than myself. I do not know that person in the world whose happiness I do not wish, and would not promote, were it in my power. In an especial manner, I love my uncle and my master; but, above all, my friend.

Mill. You have a friend, then, whom you love?

Barn. As he does me, sincerely.

Mill. He is no doubt, often blest with your company and conversation?

Barn. We live in one house together, and both serve the same worthy merchant.

Mill. Happy, happy youth! whoe'er thou art, I envy thee, and so must all, who see and know this youth. What have I lost by being formed a woman! I hate my sex, myself. Had I been a man, I might, perhaps, have been as happy in your friendship as he who now enjoys it; but, as it is—Oh!—

Barn. I never observed women before, or this is, sure, the most beautiful of her sex.—(*aside*)—You seem disordered, madam? may I know the cause?

Mill. Do not ask me,—I can never speak it, whatever is the cause; I wish for things impossible: I would be a servant bound to the same master as you are, to live in one house with you.

Barn. How strange, and yet how kind, her words and actions are—and the effect they have on me, is as strange! I feel desires I never knew before: I must begone, while I have power to go. (*aside*) Madam, I humbly take my leave.

Mill. You will not, sure, leave me so soon!
Barn. Indeed, I must.
Mill. You cannot be so cruel! I have prepared a poor supper, at which I promised myself your company.
Barn. I am sorry I must refuse the honour that you designed me; but my duty to my master calls me hence. I never yet neglected his service; he is so gentle, and so good a master, that should I wrong him, though he

might forgive me, I never should forgive myself.

Mill. Am I refused, by the first man, the second favour I ever stooped to ask? Go, then, thou proud, hard-hearted youth!—But know, you are the only man that could be found, who would let me sue twice for greater favours.

Barn. What shall I do! How shall I go or stay!

Mill. Yet do not, do not leave me! I wish my sex's pride would meet your scorn; but, when I look upon you, and behold those eyes—O, spare my tongue, and let my blushes speak! This flood of tears, too, that will force their way, and declare—what woman's modesty should hide.

Barn. O, heavens! she loves me, worthless as I am; her looks, her words, her flowing tears confess it:—and can I leave her, then? Oh, never, never! Madam, dry up those tears. You shall command me always: I will stay here for ever, if you'd have me.

Lucy. So! she has wheedled him out of his virtue of obedience already, and will strip him of all the rest, one after another, till she has left him as few as her ladyship, or myself. (*Aside.*)

Mill. Now you are kind, indeed; but I mean not to detain you always: I would have you shake off all slavish obedience to your master, but you may serve him still.

Lucy. Serve him still!—ay, or he'll have no opportunity of fingering his cash, and then he'll not serve your end, I'll be sworn. (*Aside*)

Enter BLUNT.

Blunt. Madam, supper's on the table.

Mill. Come, sir; you'll excuse all defects:—my thoughts were too much employed on my guest to observe the entertainment.

[*Exeunt* MILLWOOD *and* BARNWELL.

Blunt. What is all this preparations, this elegant supper, variety of wines, and music, for the entertainment of that young fellow?

Lucy. So it seems.

Blunt. What, is our mistress turned fool at last:—she's in love with him, I suppose?

Lucy. I suppose not,—but she designs to make him in love with her, if she can.

Blunt. What will she get by that? he seems under age, and can't be supposed to have much money.

Lucy. But his master has; and that's the same thing, as she'll manage it.

Blunt. I don't like this fooling with a handsome young fellow: while she's endeavouring to ensnare him, she may be caught herself.

Lucy. Nay, were she like me, that would certainly be the consequence; for I confess, there is something in youth and innocence that moves me mightily.

Blunt. Yes, so does the smoothness and plumpness of a partridge move a mighty desire in the hawk to be the destruction of it.

Lucy. Why, birds are their prey, as men are ours; though, as you observed, we are sometimes caught ourselves; but that, I dare say, will never be the case with our mistress.

Blunt. I wish it may prove so; for you know we all depend upon her: should she trifle away her time with a young fellow that there's nothing to be got by, we must all starve.

Lucy. There's no danger of that, for I am sure she has no view in this affair but interest.

Blunt. Well, and what hopes are there of success in that?

Lucy. The most promising that can be. 'Tis true the youth has his scruples; but she'll soon teach him to answer them, by stifling his conscience. O the lad is in a hopeful way, depend upon it. [*Exeunt.*

ACT II.

SCENE I.—*A Room in Thorowgood's House.*

Enter BARNWELL.

Barn. How strange are all things round me! Like some thief who treads forbidden ground, fearful I enter each apartment of this well known house. To guilty love, as if that was too little, already have I added breach of trust! A thief! Can I know myself that wretched thing, and look my honest friend and injured master in the face? Though hypocrisy may awhile conceal my guilt, at length it will be known, and public shame and ruin must ensue. In the mean time, what must be my life? Ever to speak a language foreign to my heart; hourly to add to the number of my crimes in order to conceal them. Sure such

was the condition of the grand apostate, when first he lost his purity; like me, disconsolate he wandered, and, while yet in heaven, bore all his future hell upon him.

Enter TRUEMAN.

True. Barnwell! O how I rejoice to see you safe! so will our master and his gentle daughter, who during your absence often inquired after you.

Barn. Would he were gone! his officious love will pry into the secrets of my soul. (*Aside.*)

True. Unless you knew the pain the whole family has felt on your account, you cannot conceive how much you are beloved; but why thus cold and silent? When my heart is full, of joy for your return, why do you turn away? Why thus avoid me? What have I done? How have I altered since you saw me last? Or rather what have you done? And why are you thus changed? For I am still the same.

Barn. What have I done, indeed? (*Aside.*)

True. Not speak nor look upon me!

Barn. By my face he will discover all I would conceal: methinks already I begin to hate him. (*Aside.*

True. I cannot bear this usage from a friend, one whom till now I have ever found so loving, whom yet I love, though his unkindness strikes at the root of friendship, and might destroy it in any breast but mine,

Barn. I am not well. (*turning to him*) Sleep has been a stranger to these eyes since you saw them last.

True. Heavy they look, indeed, and swoln with tears;—now they o'erflow; rightly did my sympathising heart forbode last night, when thou wast absent, something fatal to our peace.

Barn. Your friendship engages you too far. My troubles, whatever they are, are mine alone: you have no interest in them, nor ought your concern for me give you a moment's pain.

True. You speak as if you knew of friendship nothing but the name. Before I saw your grief, I felt it:—even now, though ignorant of the cause, your sorrow wounds me to the heart.

Barn. 'Twill not be always thus: friendship and all engagements cease, as circumstances vary; and since you once may hate me, perhaps it might be better for us both that now you love me less.

True. Sure I but dream! Without a cause would Barnwell use me thus? Ungenerous and ungrateful youth, farewell,—I shall never endeavour to follow your advice. (*going*) Yet stay, perhaps I am too rash:—prythee forgive me, Barnwell. Try to compose your ruffled mind, and let me know the cause that thus transports you from yourself; my friendly counsel may restore your peace.

Barn. All that is possible for man to do for man, your generous friendship may effect; but here even that's in vain.

True. Something dreadful is labouring in your breast. O give it vent, and let me share your grief: 'twill ease your pain, should it admit no cure; and make it lighter by the part I bear.

Barn. Vain supposition! My woes increase by being observed. Should the cause be known they would exceed all bounds.

True. So well I know thy honest heart, guilt cannot harbour there.

Barn. O torture insupportable! (*aside*)

True. Then why am I excluded?—have I a thought I would conceal from you?

Barn. If still you urge me on this hated subject, I'll never enter more beneath this roof, nor see your face again.

True. 'Tis strange,—but I have done: say but you hate me not.

Barn. Hate you! I am not that monster yet.

True. Shall our friendship still continue?

Barn. It was a blessing I never was worthy of, yet now must stand on terms, and but upon conditions can confirm it.

True. What are they?

Barn. Never hereafter, though you should wonder at my conduct, desire to know more than I am willing to reveal.

True. 'Tis hard; but upon any conditions I must be your friend.

Barn. Then, as much as one lost to himself can be another's, I am yours. (*embracing.*)

True. Be ever so, and may heaven restore your peace! But business requires our attendance; business, the youth's best preservative from ill, as idleness his worst of snares. Will you go with me?

Barn. I'll take a little time to reflect on what has past, and follow you. (*exit* TRUEMAN) I might have trusted Trueman to have applied to my uncle to have repaired the wrong I have done my master; but what of Millwood? Shall I leave her, for ever leave her, and not let her know the cause? she who loves me with such a boundless passion. Can cruelty be duty? I judge of what she then must feel, by what I now endure. How then can I determine?

Enter THOROWGOOD.

Thor. Without a cause assigned or notice given, to absent yourself last night was a fault, young man, and I came to chide you for it, but hope I am prevented; that modest blush, the confusion so visible in your face, speak grief and shame: when we have offended heaven, it requires no more; and shall man, who needs himself to be forgiven, be harder to appease? If my pardon or love be of moment to your peace, look up secure of both.

Barn. This goodness has o'ercome me. (*aside*) O, sir! you know not the nature and extent of my offence; and I should abuse your mistaken bounty to receive them. Though I had rather die than speak my shame; though racks could not have forced the guilty secret from my breast, your kindness has.

Thor. Enough, enough; whate'er it be, this concern shows you are convinced, and I am satisfied. How painful is the sense of guilt to an ingenuous mind!—some youthful folly, which it were prudent not to inquire into.

Barn. It will be known, and you recall your pardon and abhor me.

Thor. I never will! so Heaven confirm to me the pardon of my offences. Yet be upon your guard in this gay thoughtless season of your life: when vice becomes habitual, the very power of leaving it is lost.

Barn. Hear me, then, on my knees confess—

Thor. That I will not hear a syllable more upon this subject; it were not mercy, but cruelty to hear what must give you such torment to reveal.

Barn. This generosity amazes and distracts me.

Thor. This remorse makes thee dearer to me than if thou had'st never offended; whatever is your fault, of this I'm certain, 'twas harder for you to offend than me to pardon.   [*Exit.*

Barn. Villain, villain, villain! basely to wrong so excellent a man: should I again return to folly—detested thought!—but what of Millwood, then?—Why, I renounce her;—I give her up; the struggle is over, and virtue has prevailed. Reason may convince, but gratitude compels. This unlooked for generosity has saved me from destruction. (*going.*)

Enter to him a FOOTMAN.

Foot. Sir, two ladies from your uncle in the country, desire to see you.

Barn. Who should they be? (*aside*) Tell them I'll wait upon then. (*exit* FOOTMAN) Methinks I dread to see them. Guilt, what a coward hast thou made me.   [*Exit.*

SCENE II.—*Another Room in Thorowgood's House.*

Enter MILLWOOD *and* LUCY, *and to them a Footman.*

Foot. Ladies, he'll wait upon you immediately.

Mill. 'Tis very well.—I thank you.
                  [*Exit* FOOTMAN.

Enter BARNWELL.

Barn. Confusion: Millwood!

Mill. That angry look tells me that here I'm an unwelcome guest; I feared as much; the unhappy are so everywhere.

Barn. Will nothing but my utter ruin content you?

Mill. Unkind and cruel! Lost myself, your happiness is now my only care.

Barn. How did you gain admission?

Mill. Saying we were desired by your uncle to visit and deliver a message to you, we were received by the family without suspicion, and with much respect directed here.

Barn. Why did you come at all?

Mill. I never shall trouble you more; I'm come to take my leave for ever. Such is the malice of my fate. I go hopeless, despairing ever to return. This hour is all I have left me. One short hour is all I have to bestow on love and you, for whom I thought the longest life too short.

6

Barn. Then we are to part for ever?

Mill. It must be so;—yet think not that time or absence shall ever put a period to my grief, or make me love you less. Though I must leave you, yet condemn me not.

Barn. Condemn you? No, I approve your resolution, and rejoice to hear it; 'tis just,—'tis necessary,—I have well weighed, and found it so.

Lucy. I'm afraid the young man has more sense than she thought he had. (*aside.*)

Barn. Before you came I had determined never to see you more.

Mill. Confusion! (*aside.*)

Lucy. Ay! we are all out; this is a turn so unexpected, that I shall make nothing of my part; they must e'en play the scene betwixt themselves. (*aside.*)

Mill. 'Twas some relief to think, though absent, you would love me still; but to find you had resolved to cast me off—this, as I never could expect, I have not learnt to bear.

Barn. I am sorry to hear that you blame in me a resolution that so well becomes us both.

Mill. I have reason for what I do, but you have none.

Barn. Can we want a reason for parting, who have so many to wish we had never met?

Mill. Look on me, Barnwell; nay, look again:—am I not she whom yesterday you thought the fairest and the kindest of her sex?

Barn. No more; let me repent my former follies, if possible, without remembering what they are.

Mill. Why?

Barn. Such is my fraility, that 'tis dangerous.

Mill. Where is the danger, since we are to part?

Barn. The thought of that is already too painful.

Mill. If it be painful to part, then I may hope at least you do not hate me?

Barn. No,—no,—I never said I did,—O my heart!—

Mill. Perhaps you pity me!

Barn. I do,—I do,—indeed, I do.

Mill. You'll think upon me!

Barn. Doubt it not, while I can think at all.

Mill. You may judge an embrace at parting too great a favour, though it would be the last? (*he draws back*) A look shall then suffice,—farewell for ever.   [*Exit with* LUCY.

Barn. If to resolve to suffer be to conquer, I have conquered. Painful victory!

Re-enter MILLWOOD *and* LUCY.

Mill. One thing I had forgot,——I never must return to my own house again. This I thought proper to let you know, lest your mind should change, and you should seek in vain to find me there. Forgive me this second intrusion; I only came to give you this caution, and that was needless.

Barn. I hope it was, yet it is kind, and I must thank you for it.

Mill. My friend, your arm. (*to* LUCY.) Now I am gone for ever. (*going*)

Barn. One thing more:—sure there's no danger in my knowing where you go? If you think otherwise?—

Mill. Alas! (*weeping*)

Lucy. We are right, I find that's my cue.— (*aside*)—Ah, dear, sir, she's going she knows not whither; but go she must.

Barn. Humanity obliges me to wish you well: why will you expose yourself to needless troubles?

Lucy. Nay, there's no help for it: she must quit the town immediately, and the kingdom as soon as possible; it was no small matter, you may be sure, that could make her resolve to leave you.

Mill. No more, my friend; since he for whose dear sake alone I suffer, and am content to suffer, is kind and pities me. Where'er I wander, through wilds and deserts, benighted and forlorn, that thought shall give me comfort.

Barn. For my sake! O tell me how! which way am I so cursed as to bring such ruin on on thee?

Mill. To know it will but increase your troubles.

Barn. My troubles can't be greater than they are.

Lucy. Well, well, sir, if she won't satisfy you, I will.

Barn. I am bound to you beyond expression.

Mill. Remember, sir, that I desire you not to hear it.

Barn. Begin, and ease my racking expectation.

Lucy. Why, you must know, my lady here was an only child, but her parents dying while she was young, left her and her fortune, (no inconsiderable one, I assure you) to the care of a gentleman who has a good estate of his own.

Mill. Ay, ay, the barbarous man is rich enough!—but what are riches compared to love?

Lucy. For a while he performed the office of a faithful guardian, settled her in a house, hired her servants;—but you have seen in what manner she lived, so I need say no more of that.

Mill. How I shall live hereafter, Heaven knows.

Lucy. All things went on as one could wish, till, some time ago, his wife dying, he fell violently in love with his charge, and would fain have married her: now the man is neither old nor ugly, but a good personal sort of a man; but I don't how it was, she could never endure him; in short, her ill usage so provoked him,

that he brought in an account of his executorship, wherein he makes her debtor to him—

Mill. A trifle in itself, but more than enough to ruin me, whom, by this unjust account, he had stripped of all before.

Lucy. Now she, having neither money nor friend except me, who am as unfortunate as herself, he compelled her to pass his account, and give bond for the sum he demanded; but still provided handsomely for her, and continued his courtship, till being informed by his spies (truly I suspect some in her own family) that you were entertained at her house, and stayed with her all night, he came this morning raving and storming like a madman; talks no more of marriage, so there's no hopes of making up matters that way, but vows her ruin, unless she'll allow him the same favour that he supposes she granted you.

Barn. Must she be ruined, or find her refuge in another's arms?

Mill. He gave me but an hour to resolve in, that's happily spent with you; and now I go.

Barn. To be exposed to all the rigours of the various seasons; the summer's parching heat, and winter's cold; unhoused, to wander friendless through the inhospitable world, in misery and want; attended with fear and danger, and pursued by malice and revenge; would'st thou endure all this for me, and can I do nothing, nothing to prevent it?

Lucy. 'Tis really a pity there can be no way found out.

Barn. O, where are all my resolutions now!

Lucy. Now, I advised her, sir, to comply with the gentleman.

Barn. Tormenting fiend, away! I had rather perish, nay, see her perish, than have her saved by him; I will myself prevent her ruin, though with my own. A moment's patience; I'll return immediately.   [*Exit.*

Lucy. 'Twas well you came, or, by what I can perceive, you had lost him.

Mill. Hush!—he's here.

Enter BARNWELL *with a bag of money.*

Barn. What am I about to do? Now, you, who boast your reason all self-sufficient, suppose yourself in my condition, and determine for me; whether 'tis right to let her suffer for my faults, or, by this small addition to my guilt, prevent the ill effects of what has past. Here, take this, and with it purchase your deliverance; return to your house, and live in peace and safety.

Mill. So I may hope to see you there again.

Barn. Answer me not,—but fly,—lest, in the agonies of my remorse, I take again what is not mine to give, and abandon thee to want and misery.

Mill. Say but you'll come.

Barn. You are my fate, my heaven or my hell!   [*Exeunt* MILLWOOD *and* LUCY.

What have I done? Were my resolutions founded on reason, and sincerely made? why then has Heaven suffered me to fall? I sought not the occasion; and, if my heart deceives me not, compassion and generosity were my motives. But why should I attempt to reason! All is confusion, horror, and remorse; I find I am lost, cast down from all my late erected hopes, and plunged again in guilt, yet scarce know how or why—

Such undistinguished horrors rack my brain,
Like hell, the seat of darkness and of pain.
                                                [Exit.

ACT III.

Scene I.—*A Room in Thorowgood's House.*

Thorowgood *and* **Trueman** *sitting at a table with accompt books.*

Thor. Well! I have examined your accounts: they are not only just, as I have always found them, but regularly kept and fairly entered, I commend your diligence. Method in business is the surest guide. Are Barnwell's accounts ready for my inspection? he does not use to be the last on these occasions.

True. Upon receiving your orders he retired, I thought, in some confusion. If you please, I'll go and hasten him.

Thor. I'm now going to the Exchange; let him know, at my return, I expect to find him ready. [*Exeunt* Thor. *and* True.

Enter Maria, *with a book: sits and reads.*

Maria. How forcible is truth? The weakest mind, inspired with love of that, fixed and collected in itself, with indifference beholds the united force of earth and hell opposing: such souls are raised above the sense of pain, or so supported, that they regard it not. The martyr cheaply purchases his heaven. Small are his sufferings, great is his reward; not so the wretch who combats love with duty; when the mind, weakened and dissolved by the soft passion, feeble and hopeless, opposes its own desires. What is an hour, a day, a year of pain, to a whole life of tortures, such as these?

Enter Trueman.

True. O, Barnwell! O, my friend, how art thou fallen!

Maria. Ha! Barnwell! What of him? Speak, say, what of Barnwell?

True. 'Tis not to be concealed. I've news to tell you of him that will afflict your generous father, yourself, and all who knew him.

Maria. Defend us, heaven!

True. I cannot speak it. See there. (*gives a letter.*)

Maria. (*reads*) "Trueman,—I know my absence will surprise my honoured master and yourself; and the more, when you shall understand that the reason of my withdrawing, is my having embezzled part of the cash with which I was entrusted. After this, 'tis needless to inform you, that I intend never to return again: though this might have been known by examining my accounts, yet, to prevent that unnecessary trouble, and to cut off all fruitless expectations of my return, I have left this from the lost "George Barnwell."

True. Lost indeed! Yet how he should be guilty of what he here charges himself withal, raises my wonder equal to my grief. Never had youth a higher sense of virtue. Justly he thought, and as he thought he practised; never was life more regular than his; an understanding uncommon at his years; an open, generous manliness of temper; his manners easy, unaffected, and engaging.

Maria. This and much more you might have said with truth. He was the delight of every eye, and joy of every heart that knew him.

True. Since such he was, and was my friend, can I support his loss! See the fairest maid this wealthy city boasts, kindly condescends to weep for thy unhappy fate, poor ruined Barnwell!

Maria. Trueman, do you think a soul so delicate as his, so sensible of shame, can e'er submit to live slave to vice?

True. Never, never. So well I know him, I'm sure this act of his, so contrary to his nature, must have been caused by some unavoiable necessity.

Maria. Are there no means yet to preserve him?

True. O that there were! But few men recover reputation lost. A merchant never. Nor would he, I fear, though I should find him, ever be brought to look his injured master in the face.

Maria. I fear as much, and therefore would never have my father know it.

True. That's impossible!

Maria. What's the sum?

True. 'Tis considerable. I've marked it here, to show it, with the letter, to your father, at his return.

Maria. If I should supply the money, could you so dispose of that and the account, as to conceal this unhappy mismanagement from my father?

True. Nothing more easy; but can you intend it? Will you save a helpless wretch from ruin? Oh! 'twere an act worthy such exalted virtue as Maria's. Sure heaven, in mercy to my friend, inspired the generous thought.

Maria. Doubt not but I would purchase so great a happiness at a much dearer price. But how shall he be found?

True. Trust to my diligence for that. In the mean time, I'll conceal his absence from your father, or find such excuses for it, that the real cause shall never be suspected.

Maria. In attempting to save from shame one whom we hope may yet return to virtue, to heaven and you, the judges of this action, I appeal, whether I have done anything misbecoming my sex and character.

True. Earth must approve the deed, and heaven, I doubt not, will reward it.

Maria. If heaven succeed it, I am well rewarded. A virgin's fame is sullied by suspicion's slightest breath; and therefore, as this must be a secret from my father and the world, for Barnwell's sake—for mine—let it be so to him. [*Exeunt* MARIA *and* TRUEMAN.

Scene II.—*Millwood's House.*

Enter LUCY *and* BLUNT.

Lucy. Well, what do you think of Millwood's conduct now?

Blunt. I own it is surprising; I don't know which to admire most, her feigned or his real passion; though I have sometimes been afraid that her avarice would discover her; but his youth and want of experience make it the easier to impose on him.

Lucy. No, it is his love. To do him justice, notwithstanding his youth, he don't want understanding; but you men are much easier imposed on, in these affairs, than your vanity will allow you to believe. Let me see the wisest of you all as much in love with me as Barnwell is with Millwood, and I'll engage to make as great a fool of him.

Blunt. And, all circumstances considered, to make as much money of him too?

Lucy. I can't answer for that. Her artifice in making him rob his master at first, and the various stratagems by which she has obliged him to continue in that course, astonish even me, who know her so well.

Blunt. But then you are to consider that the money was his master's.

Lucy. There was the difficulty of it.—Had it been his own, it had been nothing. Were the world his, she might have it for a smile :—but those golden days are done ;—he's ruined, and Millwood's hopes of farther profit there are at an end.

Blunt. That's no more than we all expected.

Lucy. Being called by his master to make up his accounts, he was forced to quit his house and service, and wisely flies to Millwood for relief and entertainment.

Blunt. How did she receive him?

Lucy. As you would expect.—She wondered what he meant, was astonished at his impudence,—and, with an air of modesty peculiar to herself, swore so heartily that she never saw him before, that she put me out of countenance.

Blunt. That's much indeed! But how did Barnwell behave?

Lucy. He grieved, and, at length, enraged at this barbarous treatment, was preparing to be gone; and, making toward the door, showed a bag of money which he had stolen from his master,—the last he's ever like to have from thence.

Blunt. But then, Millwood?

Lucy. Ay, she, with her usual address, returned to her old arts of lying, swearing, and dissembling.—Hung on his neck, and wept, and swore 'twas meant in jest; till the easy fool, melted into tears, threw the money into her lap, and swore he had rather die than think her false.

Blunt. Strange infatuation!

Lucy. But what followed was stranger still. As doubts and fears, followed by reconcilement, ever increase love, where the passion is sincere; so in him it caused so wild a transport of excessive fondness, such joy, such grief, such pleasure, and such anguish, that nature in him seemed sinking with the weight, and the charmed soul disposed to quit his breast for hers,—just then, when every passion with lawless anarchy prevailed, and reason was in the raging tempest lost, the cruel, artful Millwood prevailed upon the wretched youth to promise what I tremble but to think on.

Blunt. I am amazed! what can it be?

Lucy. You will be more so to hear it is to attempt the life of his nearest relation and best benefactor.

Blunt. His uncle! whom we have often heard him speak of as a gentleman of a large estate and fair character in the country, where he lives!

Lucy. The same. She was no sooner possessessed of the last dear purchase of his ruin, but her avarice, insatiate as the grave, demands this horrid sacrifice.

Blunt. 'Tis time the world was rid of such a monster. There is something so horrid in murder, that all other crimes seem nothing when compared to that.—I would not be involved in the guilt of that for all the world.

Lucy. Nor I, heaven knows; therefore let us clear ourselves by doing all that is in our power to prevent it. I have just thought of a way, that to me seems probable. Will you join with me to detect this cursed design?

Blunt. With all my heart. How else shall I clear myself? He who knows of a murder intended to be committed, and does not discover it, in the eye of the law, and reason, is a murderer.

Lucy. Let us lose no time!—I'll acquaint you with the particulars as we go. [*Exeunt.*

SCENE III.—*A Walk at some distance from a Country Seat.—Lights down.*

Enter BARNWELL.

Barn. A dismal gloom obscures the face of day; either the sun has slipped behind a cloud, or journeys down the west of heaven, with more than common speed, to avoid the sight of what I'm doomed to act. Since I set forth on this accursed design, where'er I tread, methinks the solid earth trembles beneath my feet. Murder my uncle! my father's only brother! who since his death has been to me a father;—who took me up an infant, and an orphan; reared me with tenderest care, and still indulged me with most paternal fondness; yet here I stand avowed his destined murderer:—I stiffen with horror at my own impiety! 'Tis yet unperformed.—What if I quit my bloody purpose, and fly the place!—(*going, then stops*)—But whither, O whither shall I fly! My master's once friendly doors are ever shut against me; and without money Millwood will never see me more, and life is not to be endured without her; she's got such firm possession of my heart, and governs there with such despotic sway; aye, there's the cause of all my sin and sorrow: 'tis more than love; 'tis the fever of the soul, and madness of desire. In vain does nature, reason, conscience, all oppose it; the impetuous passion bears down all before it, and drives me on to lust, to theft, and murder. Oh, conscience! feeble guide to virtue, who only shows us when we go astray, but wants the power to stop us in our course. Ha! in yonder shady walk I see my uncle. He's alone. Now for my disguise.—(*plucks out a vizor*)—This is his hour of private meditation. Thus daily he prepares his soul for heaven, whilst I— But what have I to do with heaven? Ha! No struggles, conscience—

Hence! hence remorse, and ev'ry thought that's good;
The storm that lust began, must end in blood.

[*Puts on the vizor, draws a pistol, and exit.*

SCENE IV.—*A Cut Wood.*

Enter UNCLE.

Uncle. If I were superstitious, I should fear some danger lurked unseen, or death were nigh: a heavy melancholy clouds my spirits; my imagination is filled with ghastly forms of dreary graves, and bodies changed by death.

Enter GEORGE BARNWELL *at a distance.*

O death, thou strange mysterious power, seen every day, yet never understood, but by the incommunicative dead, what art thou? The extensive mind of man, that with a thought circles the earth's vast globe, sinks to the centre or ascends above the stars; that worlds exotic finds, or thinks it finds, thy thick clouds attempt to pass in vain. Lost and bewildered in the horrid gloom,—defeated, she returns more doubtful than before; of nothing certain, but of labour lost.

[*During this speech,* BARNWELL *sometimes presents the pistol, and draws it back again; at last he drops it, at which his uncle starts, and draws his sword.*

Barn. Oh, 'tis impossible.

Uncle. A man so near me, armed and masqued!

Barn. Nay, then there's no retreat.

(*Plucks a poniard from his bosom, and stabs him.*

Uncle. Oh! I am slain! All gracious heaven regard the prayer of thy dying servant. Bless, with thy choicest blessings, my dearest nephew; forgive my murderer, and take my fleeting soul to endless mercy.

(BARNWELL *throws off his mask, runs to him, and, kneeling by him, raises and chafes him.*

Barn. Expiring saint! Oh! murder, martyred uncle! Lift up your dying eyes, and view your nephew in your murderer. O do not look so tenderly upon me. Let indignation lighten from your eyes, and blast me ere you die. By heaven, he weeps, in pity of my woes. Tears,—tears, for blood. The murdered, in the agonies of death, weeps for his murderer. O, speak your pious purpose,—pronounce my pardon then, and take me with you. He would, but cannot. O why with such fond affection do you press my murdering hand! What! will you kiss me!—(*kisses his hand.*—UNCLE *groans and dies.*)—Life that hovered on his lips but till he had sealed my pardon, in that sigh expired. He's gone, for ever,—and oh! I follow. (*Swoons away upon his uncle's dead body.*) Do I still live to press the suffering bosom of the earth! Do I still breathe, and taint with my infectious breath the wholesome air? Let heaven, from its high throne, in justice or in mercy, now look down on that dear murdered saint, and me the murderer. And, if his vengeance spares, let pity strike and end my wretched being. Murder the worst of crimes, and parricide the worst of murders, and this the worst of parricides.

O, may it ever stand alone, accurst,
The last of murders, as it is the worst.

[*Exit.*

ACT IV.

SCENE I.—*A room in Thorowgood's house.*

Enter MARIA, TRUEMAN.

Maria. What news of Barnwell?

True. None. I have sought him with the greatest diligence, but all in vain.

Maria. Doth my father yet suspect the cause of his absenting himself?

True. All appeared so just and fair to him, it is not possible he ever should; but his absence will no longer be concealed. Your father's wise; and though he seems to hearken to the friendly excuses I would make for Barnwell, yet I'm afraid he regards them only as such, without suffering them to influence his judgment.

Maria. How does the unhappy youth defeat all our designs to serve him! yet I can never repent what we have done. Should he return, 'twill make his reconciliation with my father easier, and preserve him from future reproach from a malicious unforgiving world.

Enter THOROWGOOD *and* LUCY.

Thor. This woman here has given me a sad, (and, bating some circumstances) too probable account of Barnwell's defection.

Lucy. I am sorry, sir, that my frank confession of my former unhappy course of life should cause you to suspect my truth on this occasion.

Thor. It is not that; your confession has in it all the appearance of truth. (*to them*) Among other particulars, she informs me that Barnwell has been influenced to break his trust, and wrong me, at several times, of considerable sums of money; now, as I know this to be false, I would fain doubt the whole of her relation,—too dreadful to be willingly believed.

Maria. Sir, your pardon; I find myself on a sudden so indisposed, that I must retire. Poor, ruined Barnwell! Wretched, lost Maria! (*aside.*) [*Exit.*

Thor. How am I distressed on every side! Pity for that unhappy youth, fear for the life of a much valued friend—and then my child—the only joy and hope of my declining life. Her melancholy increases hourly, and give me painful apprehensions of her loss. O Trueman! this person informs me, that your friend, at the instigation of an impious woman, is gone to rob and murder his venerable uncle.

True. O execrable deed! I am blasted with the horror of the thought.

Lucy. This delay may ruin all.

Thor. What to do or think I know not; that he ever wronged me, I know is false; the rest may be so too, there is all my hope.

True. Trust not to that; rather suppose all true than lose a moment's time; even now the horrid deed may be a-doing; dreadful imagination! or it may be done, and we are vainly debating on the means to prevent what is already past.

Thor. This earnestness convinces me that he knows more than he has yet discovered. What ho! without there! who waits!

Enter a SERVANT.

Order the groom to saddle the swiftest horse, and prepare himself to set out with speed. An affair of life and death demands his diligence.—[*Exit* SERVANT.]—For you, whose behaviour, on this occasion, I have no time to commend as it deserves, I must engage your farther assistance. Return and observe this Millwood till I come. I have your direction, and will follow you as soon as possible.—[*Exit* LUCY.[—Trueman, you I am sure would not be idle on this occasion. [*Exit.*

True. He only who is a friend can judge of my distress. [*Exit.*

SCENE II.—*Millwood's house.*

Enter MILLWOOD.

Mill. I wish I knew the event of this design; the attempt without success would ruin him. Well! what have I to apprehend from that? I fear too much. The mischief being only intended, his friends, in pity of his youth, turn all their rage on me. I should have thought of that before. Suppose the deed done, then, and then only I shall be secure; or what if he returns without attempting it at all? But he is here, and I have done him wrong; his bloody hands show he has done the deed, but show he wants the prudence to conceal it.

Enter BARNWELL, *bloody.*

Barn. Where shall I hide me? Whither shall I fly to avoid the swift, unerring hand of justice?

Mill. Dismiss those fears; though thousands had pursued you to the door, yet, being entered here, you are safe as innocence; I have such a cavern, by art so cunningly contrived, that the piercing eyes of jealousy and revenge may search in vain, nor find the entrance to the safe retreat. There will I hide you if any danger's near.

Barn. O hide me from myself, if it be possible; for while I bear my conscience in my bosom, though I were hid where man's eye never saw, nor light e'er dawned, 'twere all in vain. For that inmate, that impartial judge, will try, convict, and sentence me for murder; and execute me with never-ending torments. Behold these hands all crimsoned o'er with my dear uncle's blood! Here's a sight to make a statue start with horror, or turn a living man into a statue,

Mill. Ridiculous! Then it seems you are afraid of your own shadow; or what's less than a shadow, your conscience.

Barn. Though to man unknown I did the accused act, what can we hide from heaven's omniscient eye?

Mill. No more of this stuff; what advantage have you made of his death? or what advantage may yet be made of it? Did you secure the keys of his treasure; those no doubt were about him: what gold, what jewels, or what else of value have you brought me?

Barn. Think you I added sacrilege to murder? Oh! had you seen him as his life flowed from him in a crimson flood, and heard him praying for me by the double name of nephew and of murderer; alas, alas! he knew not then that his nephew was his murderer; how would you have wished as I did, though you had a thousand years of life to come, to have given them all to have lengthened his one hour. But being dead, I fled the sight of what my hands had done, nor could I, to have gained the empire of the world, have violated by theft his sacred corpse.

Mill. Whining, preposterous, canting villain, to murder your uncle, rob him of life, nature's first, last, dear prerogative, after which there's no injury, then fear to take what he no longer wanted; and bring to me your penury and guilt. Do you think I'll hazard my reputation, nay my life, to entertain you?

Barn. Oh! Millwood! this from thee!—but I have done; if you hate me, if you wish me dead, then are you happy; for oh! 'tis sure my grief will quickly end me.

Mill. In his madness he will discover all, and involve me in his ruin: we are on a precipice from whence there's no retreat for both,—then to preserve myself. (*pauses*) There is no other way; 'tis dreadful; but reflection comes too late when danger's pressing, and there's no room for choice. It must be done. (*rings.*

Enter a SERVANT.

Fetch me an officer and seize this villain; he has confessed himself a murderer. Should I let him escape, I justly might be thought as bad as he. [*Exit* SERVANT.

Barn. O Millwood! sure thou dost not cannot mean it. Stop the messenger, upon my knees I beg you, call him back. (*kneels*) 'Tis fit I die, indeed, but not by you. I will this instant deliver myself into the hands of justice; indeed I will, for death is all I wish. But thy ingratitude so tears my wounded soul, 'tis

worse ten thousand times than death with torture.

Mill. Call it what you will, I am willing to live, and live secure; which nothing but your death can warrant. [BARNWELL *rises.*

Barn. If there be a pitch of wickedness that seats the author beyond the reach of vengeance, you must be secure. But what remains for me, but a dismal dungeon, hard-galling fetters, an awful trial, and ignominious death, justly to fall unpitied and abhorred? After death to be suspended between heaven and earth, a dreadful spectacle, the warning and horror of a gaping crowd. This I could bear, nay wish not to avoid, had it come from any but thine.

Enter BLUNT, *Officer, and Attendants.*

Mill. Heaven defend me! conceal a murderer! here, sir, take this youth into your custody: I accuse him of murder, and will appear to make good my charge. (*They seize him.*

Barn. To whom, of what, or how shall I complain! I'll not accuse her: the hand of heaven is in it, and this the punishment of lust and parricide.
Be warn'd, ye youths, who see my sad despair,
Avoid lewd women, false as they are fair
By reason guided, honest joys pursue:
The fair, to honour and to virtue true,
Just to herself, will ne'er be false to you.
By my example learn to shun my fate:
(How wretched is the man who's wise too late!)
Ere innocence and fame and life be lost,
Here purchase wisdom, cheaply, at my cost.
[*Exit, with Officers.*

Mill. Where's Lucy? why is she absent at such a time?

Blunt. Would I had been so too! Lucy will soon be here, and I hope to thy confusion, thou devil!

Mill. Insolent! this to me.

Blunt. The worse that we know of the devil is, that he first seduces to sin, and then betrays to punishment. [*Exit.*

Mill. They disapprove of my conduct—my ruin is resolved; I see my danger, but scorn it and them. I was not born to fall by such weak instruments. (*Going.*

Enter THOROWGOOD.

Thor. Where is this scandal of her own sex, and curse of ours?

Mill. What means this insolence? Whom do you seek?

Thor. Millwood.

Mill. Well, you have found her, then. I am Millwood.

Thor. Then you are the most impious wretch that e'er the sun beheld.

Mill. From your appearance, I should have expected wisdom and moderation; but your manners belie your aspect. What is your business here? I know you not.

Thor. Hereafter you may know me better; I am Barnwell's master.

Mill. Then you are master to a villain; which I think is not much to your credit.

Thor. Had he been as much above thy arts as my credit is superior to thy malice, I need not have blushed to own him.

Mill. My arts! I do not understand you, sir! If he has done amiss, what's that to me? Was he my servant, or yours? You should have taught him better.

Thor. Why should I wonder to find such uncommon impudence in one arrived to such a height of wickedness? Know, sorceress, I am not ignorant of any of your arts, by which you first deceived the unwary youth: I know how, step by step, you've led him on, reluctant and unwilling, from crime to crime, to this last horrid act, which you contrived, and, by your cursed wiles, even forced him to commit, and then betrayed him.

Mill. Ha! Lucy has got the advantage of me, and accused me first. Unless I can turn the accusation, and fix it upon her and Blunt, I am lost. (*aside*)

Thor. Had I known your cruel design sooner, it had been prevented. To see you punished as the law directs is all that now remains. Poor satisfaction! for he, innocent as he is, compared to you, must suffer too.

Mill. I find, sir, we are both unhappy in our servants. I was surprised at such ill-treatment from a gentleman of your appearance, without cause, and therefore too hastily returned it; for which I ask your pardon. I now perceive you have been so far imposed on, as to think me engaged in a former correspondence with your servant, and, some way or another, accessory to his undoing.

Thor. I charge you as the cause, the sole cause of all his guilt, and all his suffering; of all he now endures, and must endure, till a violent and shameful death shall put a dreadful period to his life and miseries together.

Mill. 'Tis very strange! but who's secure from scandal and detraction? So far from contributing to his ruin, I never spoke to him till since that fatal accident, which I lament as much as you: 'tis true, I have a servant, on whose account he has of late frequented my house; if she has abused my good opinion of her, am I to blame? Has not Barnwell done the same by you?

Thor. I hear you; pray go on.

Mill. I have been informed he had a violent passion for her, and she for him; but I always thought it innocent; I know her poor, and given to expensive pleasures. Now, who can tell but she may have influenced the amorous youth to commit the murder, to supply her extravagancies? It must be so: I now recollect a thousand circumstances that confirm it: I'll have her and a man servant, that I suspect as

an accomplice, secured immediately. I hope, sir, you will lay aside your ill-grounded suspicions of me, and join to punish the real contrivers of this bloody deed. (*offers to go*)

Thor. Madam, you pass not this way: I see your design, but shall protect them from your malice.

Mill. I hope you will not use your influence, and the credit of your name, to screen such guilty wretches. Consider, sir! the wickedness of persuading a thoughtless youth to such a crime.

Thor. I do,—and of betraying him when it was done.

Mill. That which you call betraying him, may convince you of my innocence. She who loves him, though she contrived the murder, would never have delivered him into the hands of justice, as I, struck with horror of his crimes, have done.

Thor. Those whom subtlely you would accuse, you know are your accusers; and, what proves unanswerably their innocence and your guilt, they accused you before the deed was done, and did all that was in their power to have prevented it.

Mill. Sir, you are very hard to be convinced; but I have such a proof, which, when produced, will silence all objections. [*Exit.*

Enter LUCY, TRUEMAN, BLUNT, *Officers, &c.*

Lucy. Gentlemen, pray place yourselves, some on one side of that door, and some on the other: watch her entrance, and act as your prudence directs you. This way—(*to* THOROWGOOD)—She's driven to the last extremity, and is forming some desperate resolution. I guess at her design.

Enter MILLWOOD *with a pistol,* TRUEMAN *secures her.*

True. Here thy power of doing mischief ends; deceitful, cruel, bloody woman!

Mill. Fool, hypocrite, villain, man! thou canst not call me that.

True. To call thee woman, were to wrong the sex, thou devil!

Mill. That imaginary being is an emblem of thy cursed sex collected; a mirror, wherein each particular man may see his own likeness, and that of all mankind.

True. Think not by aggravating the faults of others to extenuate thy own, of which the abuse of such uncommon perfections of mind and body is not the least.

Mill. If such I had, well may I curse your barbarous sex, who robbed me of them, ere I knew their worth; then left me, too late, to count their value by their loss. Another and another spoiler came, and all my gain was poverty and reproach. My soul disdained, and yet disdains, dependence and contempt. Riches,

13

no matter by what means obtained, I saw secured the worst of men from both: I found it therefore necessary to be rich; and, to that end, I summoned all my arts. You call them wicked: be it so; they were such as my conversation with your sex had furnished me withal.

Thor. Sure none but the worst of men conversed with thee.

Mill. Men of all degrees and all professions I have known, yet found no difference, but in their several capacities; all were alike wicked to the utmost of their power. In pride, contention, avarice, cruelty, and revenge, the reverend priesthood were my unerring guides. From suburb magistrates, who live by ruined reputations, as the unhospitable natives of Cornwall do by shipwrecks, I learned that to charge my innocent neighbours with my crimes was to merit their protection; for to screen the guilty is the less scandalous, when many are suspected; and detraction, like darkness and death, blackens all objects, and levels all distinction. Such are your venal magistrates, who favour none but such as, by their office, are sworn to punish: with them not to be guilty, is the worst of crimes; and large fees, privately paid, are every needful virtue.

Thor. Your practice has sufficiently discovered your contempt of laws, both humane and divine; no wonder, then, that you should hate the officers of both.

Mill. I hate you all; I know you, and expect no mercy; nay, I ask for none. I have done nothing that I am sorry for; I followed my inclinations, and that the best of you does every day. All actions are alike natural and indifferent to man and beast, who devour, or are devoured, as they meet with others weaker or stronger than themselves.

Thor. What pity it is, a mind so comprehensive, daring, and inquisitive, should be a stranger to religion's sweet, but powerful charms!

Mill. I am not fool enough to be an Atheist, though I have known enough of men's hypocrisy to make a thousand simple women so. Whatever religion is in itself, as practised by mankind, it has caused the evil you say it was designed to cure. War, plague, and famine, have not destroyed so many of the human race, as this pretended piety has done; and with such barbarous cruelty, as if the only way to honour heaven were to turn the present world into hell.

Thor. Truth is truth, though from an enemy and spoke in malice. You bloody, blind, and superstitious bigots, how will you answer this?

Mill. What are your laws of which you make your boast, but the fool's wisdom, and the coward's valour; the instrument and screen of all your villanies, by which you punish in others what you act yourselves, or would have acted, had you been in their circumstances. The judge who condemns the poor man for being a thief, had been a thief himself had he been poor. Thus you go on deceiving, and being deceived, harassing, and plaguing, and destroying one another! but women are your universal prey.

Women, by whom you are the source of joy,
With cruel arts you labour to destroy:
A thousand ways our ruin you pursue,
Yet blame in us those arts first taught by you.
O may, from hence, each violated maid,
By flattering, faithless, barb'rous man betray'd:
When robb'd of innocence, and virgin fame,
From your destruction raise a nobler name;
To right their sex's wrongs devote their mind,
And future Millwoods prove, to plague mankind.

[*Exeunt.*

ACT V.

SCENE I.—*A Dungeon, a Table and Lamp,* BARNWELL, *reading.*

Enter THOROWGOOD.

Thor. See there the bitter fruits of passion's detested reign, and sensual appetite indulged— severe reflections, penitence, and tears.

Barn. My honoured, injured master, forgive this last unwilling disrespect,—indeed, I saw you not.

Thor. 'Tis well; I hope you were better employed in viewing of yourself;—I sent a reverend divine to teach you to improve it, and should be glad to hear of his success.

Barn. The word of truth, which he recommended for my constant companion in this my sad retirement, has at length removed the doubts I laboured under. From thence I've learned the infinite extent of heavenly mercy; that my offences, though great, are not unpardonable; and that it is not my interest only, but my duty to believe, and to rejoice in that hope;—so shall heaven receive the glory, and future penitents the profit of my example.

Thor. Go on. How happy am I who live to see this!

Barn. 'Tis wonderful, that words should charm despair, speak peace and pardon to a murderer's conscience;—but truth and mercy flow in every sentence, attended with force and energy divine. How shall I describe my present state of mind? I hope in doubt—and trembling I rejoice. I feel my grief increase, even as my fears give way. Joy and gratitude now supply more tears than the horror and anguish of despair before.

Thor. These are the genuine signs of true repentance—the only preparatory certain way to everlasting peace.

Barn. What do I owe for all your generous kindness! but though I cannot, heaven can and will reward you.

Thor. To see thee thus, is joy too great for words. Farewell.—Heaven strengthen thee!—Farewell.

Barn. O! sir, there's something I could say, if my sad swelling heart would give me leave.

Thor. Give it vent a while, and try.

Barn. I had a friend,—'tis true I am unworthy, yet methinks your generous example might persuade;—could I not see him once before I go from whence there's no return?

Thor. He's coming,—and as much thy friend as ever; but I'll not anticipate his sorrow,—too soon he'll see the sad effect of this contagious ruin. I must retire to indulge a weakness I find impossible to overcome. (*aside*) Much loved, and much lamented youth,—Farewell. Heaven strengthen thee!—eternally farewell.

Barn. The best of masters and of men—Farewell. While I live let me not want your prayers.

Thor. Thou shalt not;—thy peace being made with heaven, death is already vanquished. Bear a little longer the pains that attend this transitory life, and cease from pain for ever.
[*Exit.*

Barn. I find a power within that bears my soul above the fears of death, and, spite of conscious shame and guilt, gives me a taste of pleasure more than mortal.

Enter TRUEMAN.

Barn. Trueman,—my friend, whom I so wished to see! yet now he's here I dare not look upon him. (*weeps.*)

True. O Barnwell! Barnwell!

Barn. Mercy! Mercy! gracious heaven! For death, but not for this, was I prepared.

True. What have I suffered since I saw you last!—what pain has absence given me!—But oh! to see thee thus!

Barn. I know it is dreadful! I feel the anguish of thy generous soul; but I was born to murder all who love me. (*Both weep.*)

True. I came not to reproach you;—I thought to bring you comfort. O had you trusted me when first the fair seducer tempted you, all might have been prevented.

Barn. Alas, thou knowest not what a wretch I've been. Breach of friendship was my first

and least offence. So far was I lost to goodness: so devoted to the author of my ruin;—that had she insisted on my murdering thee, I think I should have done it.

True. Prythee aggravate thy faults no more.

Barn. I think I should!—thus good and generous as you are, I should have murdered you!

True. We have not yet embraced, and may be interrupted. Come to my arms.

Barn. Never, never will I taste such joys on earth; never will I so soothe my just remorse. Are those honest arms and faithful bosom fit to embrace and to support a murderer? These iron fetters only shall clasp, and flinty pavement bear me;—even these too good for such a bloody monster.

True. Shall fortune sever those whom friendship joined? Thy miseries cannot lay thee so low, but love will find thee. Upon this rugged couch then let us lie, for well it suits our most deplorable condition. Here will we offer to stern calamity,—this earth the altar, and ourselves the sacrifice. Our mutual groans shall echo to each other through the dreary vault. Our sighs shall number the moments as they pass, and mingling tears communicate such anguish, as words were never made to express.

Barn. Since you propose an intercourse of woe, pour all your griefs into my breast, and in exchange take mine.—(*embracing*)—Where's now the anguish that you promised? You have taken mine, and make me no return. Sure peace and comfort dwell within these arms, and sorrow cannot reproach me while I am here! This, too, is the work of heaven, who, having before spoken peace and pardon to me, now sends thee to confirm it. O take, take some of the joy that overflows my breast!

Enter KEEPER.

Keeper. Sir.

True. I come.

Barn. Must you leave me! Death would soon have parted us for ever.

True. O, my Barnwell, there is yet another task behind; again your heart must bleed for others' woes.

Barn. To meet and part with you I thought was all I had to do on earth! What is there more for me to do or suffer!

True. I dread to tell thee, yet it must be known! Maria—

Barn. Our master's fair and virtuous daughter!

True. The same.

Barn. No misfortune, I hope, has reached that lovely maid! Preserve her heaven, from every ill, to show mankind that goodness is your care.

True. Whatever you and I have felt, and more, if more be possible, she feels for you.

15

Barn. This is, indeed, the bitterness of death! (*aside.*)

True. You must remember, for we all observed it, for some time past, a heavy melancholy weighed her down. Disconsolate she seemed, and pined and languished from a cause unknown; till, hearing of your dreadful fate, the long-stifled flame blazed out, and in the transport of her grief, discovered her own lost state, while she lamented yours.

Barn. (*weeping*) Why did not you let me die and never know it?

True. It was impossible; she makes no secret of her passion for you, and is determined to see you ere you die; she waits for me to introduce her.   [*Exit.*

Barn. Vain, busy thoughts, be still! What avails it to think on what I might have been? —I now am—What I have made myself.

Enter TRUEMAN *and* MARIA.

True. Madam, reluctant I lead you to this dismal scene: this is the seat of misery and guilt. Here awful justice reserves her public victims. This is the entrance to shameful death.

Maria. To this sad place then, no improper guest, the abandoned lost Maria brings despair: —and see the subject and the cause of all this world of woe. Silent and motionless he stands, as if his soul had quitted her abode, and the lifeless form alone was left behind.

Barn. Just heaven, I am your own: do with me what you please.

Maria. Why are your streaming eyes still fixed below, as though thou'dst give the greedy earth thy sorrows, and rob me of my due? Where happiness within your power, you should bestow it where you pleased; but in your misery I must and will partake.

Barn. Oh! say not so, but fly, abhor, and leave me to my fate. Consider what you are: so shall I quickly be to you as though I had never been.

Maria. When I forget you I must be so indeed. Reason, choice, virtue, all forbid it. Let women, like Millwood, if there be more such women, smile in prosperity, and in adversity forsake. Be it the pride of virtue to repair, or to partake, the ruin such have made.

True. Lovely, ill-fated maid!

Maria. Yes, fruitless is my love, and unavailing all my sighs and tears. Can they save thee from approaching death?—from such a death! O sorrow insupportable!

Barn. Preserve her heaven, and restore her peace; nor let her death be added to my crimes!—(*bell rings*)—I am summoned to my fate.

Enter KEEPER.

Keeper. The officers attend you, sir. Millwood is already summoned.   [*Exit.*

Barn. Tell them I am ready. And now, my friend, farewell.—(*embracing*)—Support and comfort the best you can this mourning fair. No more. Forget not to pray for me.— (*crosses to* MARIA)—Would you, bright excellence, permit me the honour of a chaste embrace, the last happiness this world could give were mine.—(*she inclines towards him; they embrace*)—Exalted goodness! O turn your eyes from earth and me, to heaven, where virtue, like yours, is ever heard. Pray for the peace of my departing soul. Early my race of wickedness began, and soon has reached the summit. Ere nature has finished her work, and stamped me man, just at the time that others begin to stray, my course is finished. Though short my span of life, and few my days, yet count my crimes for years and I have lived whole ages. Justice and mercy are in heaven the same: its utmost severity is mercy to the whole,—thereby to cure man's folly and presumption, which else would render even infinite mercy vain and ineffectual. Thus justice, in compassion to mankind, cuts off a wretch like me, by one such example to secure thousands from future ruin.

If any youth like you, in future times,
Shall mourn my fate, though he abhor my
      crimes;
Or tender maid, like you, my tale shall hear,
And to my sorrows give a pitying tear:
To each such melting eye, and throbbing heart,
Would gracious heaven this benefit impart,
Never to know my guilt, nor feel my pain,
Then must you own you ought not to complain;
Since you nor weep, nor shall I die, in vain.

END OF "GEORGE BARNWELL."